Molly & the Good Shepherd

Written by Chris Auer
Illustrated by Amy Wummer

512305

Zonderkidz

For Barbara, Babs, and Dolly. Thank you for your friendship.

C.A.

To everyone who's been lost, then found.

A.W.

Zonder**kidz**®

The children's group of Zondervan

www.zonderkidz.com

Molly & the Good Shepherd
Copyright © 2005 by Chris Auer
Illustrations copyright © 2005 by Amy Wummer

Reproduced by permission of Adelia C. Rasines/Newington Cropsey Foundation, *The Good Shepherd* (28" x 44"),
1855 by Jasper F. Cropsey. Photo by Jerry L. Thompson.

Requests for information should be addressed to:
Grand Rapids, Michigan 49530

Library of Congress Cataloging-in-Publication Data

Auer, Chris, 1955-
  Molly and the Good Shepherd / by Chris Auer.-- 1st ed.
      p. cm.
  Summary: When Molly gets lost in a museum during a school field trip, she finds a guard who talks to her about a painting
of the Good Shepherd while they wait for her teacher to come for her.
  ISBN 0-310-70826-5 (hardcover)
  [1. Lost children--Fiction. 2. School field trips--Fiction. 3. Museums--Fiction. 4. Jesus Christ--Art--Fiction. 5. Conduct of
life--Fiction.] I. Title.

PZ7.A9113Mol 2005
[Fic]--dc22
                                                                                    2004000192

Zonderkidz is a trademark of Zondervan
Editor: Amy DeVries
Interior design and art direction: Laura M. Maitner

Printed in China
05 06 07 08/LPC/5 4 3 2 1

"I am the good shepherd. I know my sheep, and my sheep know me."

John 10:14

When Molly woke up she knew it was a special day, but it took her a minute to remember why.

"That's right!" she said. "Today is the day my class is going on a field trip to the city!"

For a week, Molly and her friends in the third grade talked again and again about the museum they would visit. They were very excited.

Molly jumped out of bed and got dressed. She took care to put on the red T-shirt with the big letters that said "Fuller Elementary School." There was also a picture of a rabbit—the school mascot.

"Remember, Molly," her mother reminded her, "be like the rabbit and put on your listening ears today."

Sometimes Molly didn't pay as much attention to her teacher as she should.

olly laughed when she got to school. Her classroom was a sea of red. Even their teacher, Miss O'Hara, wore a red shirt.

"Class!" Miss O'Hara called out. "It's important that you stay together and with your buddy."

That made Molly feel sad. Her best friend, Ellen, was sick, and since all the other girls had buddies, Miss O'Hara said Molly and Ben should be buddies. Ben was not Molly's favorite person in the class. In fact, he teased Molly the most. Ellen said it was because Ben liked Molly. But Molly thought it was because Ben liked to make noise.

The bus drove down winding back roads away from Molly's school, then along an eight-lane highway, and finally over an enormous steel bridge that crossed a wide river. The city was on the other side of the river.

Molly never saw so many people in one place. The big city made her feel very small and unimportant. She was glad to have Ben next to her as her buddy—even though he was talking to everyone on the bus but her.

The bus pulled up to the front of the museum. There were tall columns all along the front of the museum, and all along the inside of the huge lobby too. Everything was made of shiny marble and granite.

When Molly talked, she heard an echo, just like the inside of a cave. Ben was making noises just so he could hear the echo, but Miss O'Hara made him stop.

Down a long hallway, Molly saw a tall statue of a man holding a sword. At the top of a wide staircase was a huge painting of a battle. Even before Miss O'Hara told the students to take a buddy's hand and follow her, Molly took Ben's hand and held on tight. She wondered how she could feel like smiling and crying at the same time.

Molly wasn't sure when she let go of Ben's hand. Maybe it was in front of the painting of a beautiful castle she wanted to look at for a minute longer. Or maybe it was when the rest of the class went on to the room with the statues, but she wanted to take one more look at the picture of the girl with the umbrella.

Molly forgot to be afraid. And as she walked from one painting to another, she also forgot Miss O'Hara's words about staying together. Suddenly, Molly turned and looked around. She couldn't see a single red shirt anywhere. Now she was afraid.

At the top of the staircase, Miss O'Hara and the other adults who were helping her with the class counted the students to make sure they were all there. But something was wrong. Someone was missing.

"Where's Molly?" asked Miss O'Hara.

Ben didn't know. He and his friend Ian had been giggling as they gave the statues funny names like "Durwood" and "Hazel." But Ben wasn't laughing now. Like everyone else, he was worried about Molly.

Molly blinked back tears. She knew this was not a good time to cry. She had to think. She tried to remember what Miss O'Hara said to do if she got lost. Why wasn't she a better listener?

"Find an adult in a uniform and ask for help!" Molly said loudly as she remembered her teacher's words. She looked around. At the far end of the room was a guard in uniform. He was there to help. Molly ran to him as fast as she could.

iss O'Hara left her students with the other adults. She ran down the wide staircase and across the long hall. She looked for a guard. Maybe a guard could help her find Molly.

One guard was standing behind a tall statue. Miss O'Hara did not see her. Another guard disappeared around a corner before Miss O'Hara could catch up with him.

Like Molly, Miss O'Hara was scared. She knew one of her little ones was in trouble, so she said a quick prayer asking God to protect Molly. Then she took a deep breath and went on looking for help.

ello, my name is Molly and I'm lost! Can you help me?"

"Hello, Molly," the guard answered, "My name is Antonio, and I'd be glad to help you."

Just being near Antonio made Molly feel better. He spoke to someone through his walkie-talkie, and then took her hand while they waited for an answer.

Molly looked at the painting on the wall across from where they stood. It was the most beautiful one she had seen so far. It seemed as if someone had painted a picture of heaven. And the man who stood with the sheep—yes, she was sure it was Jesus.

"This is my favorite picture in the whole museum," said Antonio. "I always feel better when I look at it."

The Lord is my shepherd. He gives me everything I need," recited Molly as she gazed at the painting.

"That's right!" exclaimed Antonio.

"I am the Good Shepherd," she added. "Jesus said that."

"Do you know what it means?" asked Antonio.

"Not really. But I know it's something I heard in church. Sometimes I don't listen as well as I should."

"Well," Antonio explained, "sheep are soft and sweet and wonderful. But they can get into a lot of trouble if there is no one watching over them. They need a shepherd."

"Someone to take care of them," whispered Molly.

"Yes. That's what Jesus meant when he said he was the Good Shepherd. If we really listen to him, we can stay out of trouble."

Tears stung Molly's eyes. Antonio knelt down and gave her a hug.

"It's okay. Sometimes the sheep that gets lost is the one that loves the shepherd most."

A moment later, Miss O'Hara hurried around the corner and almost ran into Molly and Antonio.

"There you are!" she exclaimed. "Oh, Molly, I've been looking everywhere for you!"

Molly gave her teacher a hug. Antonio used his walkie-talkie to report the good news.

"Remember," said Antonio to Molly with a wink. Then he touched his ear to remind her of something.

"I will!" Molly called out as she waved goodbye.

"Remember what?" asked Miss O'Hara.

"Remember that I was given ears for a reason," answered Molly as she held on tightly to her teacher's hand.

By the time the school bus crossed the bridge and left the city behind, Molly was fast asleep. Ben sat quietly beside her until he too fell asleep. Soon the whole bus was quiet as all the children slept.

Miss O'Hara looked back at them and smiled. Each and every one of her students was precious to her. Each and every one belonged to the Good Shepherd, and she made a silent promise to help him take care of them.

Jasper F. Cropsey painted *The Good Shepherd* in 1855. He was inspired by the Twenty-third Psalm. Cropsey was one of several American painters who loved God and tried to reflect his glory in the landscapes they painted.

These artists were part of a movement known as the Hudson River School because many of them lived near that famous river in New York State, and often featured it in their paintings.

Mr. Cropsey strove at all times to honor God with his talents and to show others the richness of God's creation. *The Good Shepherd* is owned by Jasper F. Cropsey's great-granddaughter, Mrs. John C. Newington.